LILA & THE DARK

Book 1

Chris Ross

CRBooks.ink

Book Cover by Chris Ross

Illustrations by Chris Ross

First edition edition 2024

Paperback ISBN: 9798330517336

eBook ISBN: 9798330517343

CONTENTS

Dedication — V

Epigraph — VI

1. The Girl in the Shadows — 1

2. From Fear to Friendship — 6

3. Shadows of Trust — 9

4. The Name of the Night — 12

5. Secrets in the Shadows — 16

6. Shadows of War — 19

7. The Eternal Choice — 22

8. Shadows Reborn — 26

9. Embrace of the Night — 29

10. Reckoning Shadows — 32

11. Journey Through the Night's Veil — 36

12. Thank You — 40

About the author   43

Coming Soon: City & Shadows   45

To my father, a man who taught me the true strength lies not in perfection, but in the courage to rise after every fall. Your journey from a good father to the best one I could ever ask for has shown me the path to becoming a better person. This book is dedicated to you, my hero, who embraced imperfections and transformed them into lessons of resilience and love.

Chris Ross

"Though my soul may set in darkness, it will rise in perfect light; I have loved the stars too fondly to be fearful of the night."

- Sarah Williams

Chapter One

THE GIRL IN THE SHADOWS

Lila pressed her forehead against the cool glass of the window, eyes tracing the gas lamps' soft glow as it spilled over the cobblestone streets of the town below. The lamps, little more than distant stars fallen to earth, fought back the encroaching night with a tender, flickering light. With each passing moment, the shadows stretched longer, whispering of hidden things that moved with the dark.

In the sanctuary of her room, candles flickered like captive fireflies, casting a warm, golden light that danced across the walls. These flames, alive and restless, stood guard around Lila, their light a shield against the thickening darkness that seemed almost alive, pressing its face against the window, curious and cold.

Her mother's voice, a familiar melody of caution, often scolded her for the extravagance of so many lit wicks.

"Now Lila, let's mind how many candles we light," her mother's voice carried a tender advisory. "We mustn't let all that wax and wick go to waste."

Yet, to Lila, each candle was a soldier in her army against the dark, a beacon to ward off the creeping dread that slithered in with the shadows—a fear not just of the physical darkness, but of the looming uncertainties their country faced.

Tonight, silence settled heavily upon the house. The last candle guttered and died, its final breath a whisper of smoke in the still air. Her mother's words, firmer now, cut through the darkness. "It's time, Lila."

The night, void of any light, waited expectantly. Wrapped tight in her blanket, Lila faced the void, her heart pounding a frantic rhythm. Despite her fear, she couldn't help but feel a strange pull towards the unknown, a curiosity that whispered back at the darkness.

The room, now a stage for the play of moonlight and shadow, whispered secrets through the rustle of the curtains. A sliver of moonlight, bold and brash, cut a path through the gloom, a fleeting comfort. Shadows danced at the corners of her vision, each one a specter of fear conjured from the depths of her imagination.

A whisper, softer than the sigh of the night wind, broke the silence. "Who...Who's there?" Lila's voice, stronger than she felt, challenged the darkness.

In response, a voice emerged from the shadows, a sound as elusive and enveloping as the night itself. "It's me... The Dark."

From the shadows, a figure materialized, strands of inky black hair framing the face of a girl, not much older than Lila. The darkness crafted a silhouette around her of both elegance and enigma. Her skin, in stark contrast to the shadowy fabric of her attire, gleamed with the luster of moonlit porcelain. Yet, it was her eyes that held Lila captive—a depth there not of void but of the night sky itself, speckled with unseen stars, promising the comfort of the unseen rather than the fear of the unknown.

The girl, sensing Lila's apprehension, paused, offering a gesture of peace with an open hand. "I mean you no harm," she assured, her voice a melody of earnestness and curiosity. Her tone held the gentle firmness of night's embrace—undeniable yet protective, like the sky cradling the earth in darkness, not to consume it, but to nurture the world to rest and rejuvenation. "I merely wish to ask you something."

Lila, drawn into the compelling aura of the girl before her, felt a calming reassurance in the earnest timbre of her voice. "Wh-What do you wish to know?" she inquired, her apprehension dissolving into the night like mist at sunrise, giving way to a blossoming curiosity that felt as if it had been waiting, just beneath the surface, for such a question.

The girl, her form a blend of shadow and light, regarded Lila with a gentle curiosity that seemed as old as the night itself. "Why does the dark stir such fear within you?" she asked, her voice not demanding but inviting, her question floating between them. It felt like an invitation to explore the depths of Lila's unease—a question echoing the uncertainties of the world outside Lila's window.

Lila felt a lump form in her throat, the past looming large and shadowy at the edge of her consciousness. There was a moment's pause, a heartbeat of silence in which Lila's eyes flickered away, caught in the internal debate of revealing her vulnerability. Then, with a heavy sigh that seemed to carry the weight of her fears, she relented, opening the gates to a memory long guarded in the shadows of her heart.

"Once, as a child, curiosity led me beyond the warmth of my home into the fading light. The world turned unfamiliar, cloaking me in a shroud of darkness so complete, I lost my way. Alone and frightened, I was too weak to call for help as the night closed in," Lila's voice wavered, a testament to the rawness of the memory. "It was my parents who found me, their lanterns piercing the darkness, guiding me back to safety. Since then, the night has felt like a vast, uncharted territory, where I once found myself lost and powerless."

The Dark listened intently, a softness in her demeanor. With a voice kind and oddly enlightening, she replied, "The shadows that haunt you, the mysteries that unsettle you, they are not born of the night. The same things that walk in the daylight are there in the dark; they are merely harder to see. The night does not change their nature, only how you perceive them."

Bathed in the moon's tender glow, a dialogue blossomed between them, weaving a tapestry of insights that promised to peel back the night's veils. This exchange, rich with revelation, was set to transform Lila's apprehension into a vibrant curiosity, forging an unexpected kinship with the darkness.

CHAPTER TWO

FROM FEAR TO FRIENDSHIP

Wrapped in the cocoon of her blankets, Lila's gaze drifted towards the Dark, her eyes flickering with a mix of curiosity and an echo of her old fears.

"Why do you linger in the shadows?" Her question, tinged with a quiver of newfound curiosity, sought to uncover the mysteries of her enigmatic friend.

The Dark Girl, illuminated softly by the moon's embrace, seemed to ponder the question. "I don't linger," she corrected gently, her voice harmonizing with the night. "With night's arrival, I am whole. My essence is not to outshine but to be, woven into the very fabric of the dark. Fear, however, casts long shadows over many hearts, veiling the path to understanding."

Lila pondered this for a moment. "I suppose my fear arises from the lack of clarity in darkness. In its veil, my imagination conjures terrifying things."

With a nod of understanding, the Dark replied, "It is a common sentiment. However, the unseen need not always be feared. Darkness often harbors wonders invisible in daylight—like the stars that reveal themselves only at night or the dreams that visit your slumber."

A new perspective began to dawn on Lila, illuminating her thoughts. "I've never seen it that way. But why...why do you look like a girl, like me?"

A smile touched the Dark's lips, gentle and revealing. "I appear in the form that those I visit are most willing to see. In your heart, despite your fears, this is how you imagined me—a reflection not of the dark itself, but of your perception within it."

Lila felt a flush of apology for her initial fear. "I'm sorry for being afraid," she whispered, a confession to the night.

The Dark Girl reached out her hand, cool yet comforting against Lila's. "There's no need for apologies, Lila. Fear is part of being human. But now that you know me, perhaps you'll find the darkness less intimidating."

Their conversation meandered like a night breeze, sharing secrets and wonders of the nocturnal world. The Dark spoke of the creatures that roamed unseen, the changing face of the moon, and the celestial stories woven among the stars. She recounted tales of ancient times when humanity embraced the night, gathering under the embrace of starlight for tales of adventure and mystery.

In return, Lila shared her world of sunlight—games played in open fields, stories that leaped from the pages of her books, and the comforting warmth of daylight. This exchange bridged their worlds, knitting together understanding and friendship beneath the watchful gaze of the moon.

As their conversation lulled, a comfortable silence settled between them. Lila found herself lost in thought, mulling over the newfound insights the Dark had shared with her.

As the first hints of dawn began to color the sky, the Dark's form grew fainter. "The morning approaches. Would you like me to return with the next nightfall?"

Lila's answer came swiftly, her voice full of eagerness. "You'd come back?"

"With every sunset, if you wish," the Dark promised, a certainty in her voice that felt like an anchor in the shifting sands of night.

A smile, wide and hopeful, spread across Lila's face. "Then it's a promise."

Laughter, light, and echoing, filled the room as the Dark's form dissipated, leaving behind the promise of future nights filled with shared discoveries. From that moment, Lila no longer greeted the evening with fear but with anticipation, ready to uncover the mysteries of the night with her enigmatic friend.

CHAPTER THREE

SHADOWS OF TRUST

As the night deepened, wrapping the world in its silent embrace, Lila sat wrapped in her blanket, her room bathed in the gentle luminescence of moonlight. She watched with bated breath as the familiar, comforting silhouette of The Dark formed from the gathering shadows, a nightly ritual that had become the heart of her evenings.

"Good evening, Lila," The Dark greeted, her voice a melody woven from the nocturne of an unseen world, echoing the joy of reunion.

Illuminated by the soft glow, Lila's face lit up with an eager smile. "I've waited all day for this," she confessed, her words tinged with the excitement of shared secrets and the anticipation of another night's adventures.

Their laughter and tales filled the room, as lively as the dance of flames in a hearth. They reveled in games of shadows and stories spun from dreams, conjuring an imaginary feast under the vigilant eyes of the stars, a celebration of their friendship.

However, as the night marched on, a gentle weariness began to veil Lila's vibrant eyes, each blink slower than the last. The Dark, ever observant, noted the change with a softness in her tone. "Lila, the embrace of sleep grows near."

Lila's words were barely above a whisper, "I don't want these moments to end. Every night with you is a treasure," she murmured, fighting the pull of sleep.

The Dark approached, her presence a comforting shade in the moonlit room. "I know, dear Lila, but rest is as important as our adventures. While you sleep, I'll watch over the coming dawn," she reassured, her voice the gentle caress of night wind through leaves. "Even in rest, you're not alone—I'll guard your slumber until the first light of morning."

A moment of silence hung in the air, filled with the unspoken understanding of their bond. Lila, comforted by The Dark's promise, allowed a small smile to grace her lips. "Promise you'll be here until the dawn?"

"Until the first light," The Dark affirmed, her presence steadfast in the waning hours of the night. "Every night, until the edge of morning."

With that assurance, Lila found solace in The Dark's unwavering dedication. As she drifted into sleep, The Dark remained a silent guardian, ensuring the tranquility of the night until the earliest signs of dawn began to light the sky, marking the time for her departure.

Chapter Four

The Name of the Night

Under the cloak of a moonlit night, in the quietude that filled Lila's room, an air of contemplation settled between the two figures bathed in silver light. Lila, a silhouette of curiosity and anticipation, broke the silence with a gentle, reflective tone.

"I realize I've never asked, and I'm sorry for that. Do you have a name?"

Lila's apology, sincere and softly spoken, bridged the gap of countless nights spent in shared secrecy and discovery.

The Dark, whose presence had become as familiar to Lila as the stars to the night sky, paused. In the stillness, her form seemed to ponder, a shadow contemplating its essence.

"Across time, in whispers and in legends, I've been known by many names," she began, her voice a mirror to the quietude of the night, resonating with the depth of untold stories.

Intrigued, Lila leaned closer, the moon casting its serene glow over her eager face, "Could you share some with me?"

Her question, laden with the weight of newfound understanding, invited The Dark to reveal the tapestry of her existence.

"With each era, each civilization, I've been a reflection of their fears, their reverence, a part of the night's infinite tapestry. In ancient Greece, they called me Nyx, the night's very soul, mother to the cosmos's wonders."

"In the lands of Spain, I was whispered as Sombra, embodying the mystery that dances just beyond the reach of light."

The room itself seemed to hold its breath, cradling the echo of names that traversed the spectrum of human emotion and imagination.

"In the verdant depths of Eastern folklore, I was revered as Yami, a whisper of the night's embrace, guarding secrets and guiding souls through the unseen, a testament to the quiet power and mystique of darkness."

"And within the empire of Rome, I bore the name Tenebra, a shroud over the unseen, the depth of the unknown that beckons the curious and the brave."

Each name that The Dark revealed wove a richer narrative, painting her not just as a figure of the night but as a constant companion to those who dared to look beyond their fears.

Lila's laughter, tinged with awe and affection, filled the space between them. "Such mystery in those names, each a world within a word."

The Dark's smile, unseen but deeply felt, acknowledged the shared joy of their discovery.

"The night, in all its mystery and beauty, is where fear and wonder meet. As Selene, I was the moon's gentle guardian, a guiding light in the darkness."

"And as Nocturna," she added, her voice a soft caress, "I celebrated the hidden wonders, the life that thrives in the embrace of shadows."

Lila, her imagination alight with visions of The Dark in all her guises, ventured further. "What about the raven, a symbol of prophecy and guardianship in many tales?"

"Indeed," The Dark affirmed, her essence a bridge between the ancient and the eternal. "As Raven, I was the keeper of secrets, the messenger between worlds, ever-watchful, ever-present."

Captivated, Lila found herself pondering the essence of a name. "With so many names, each a chapter of your vast existence, do you hold one closer to your heart?"

Looking out into the night, as if drawing inspiration from the endless dance of stars and shadows, The Dark found her answer.

"While each name has its place in my journey, one resonates with the song of the cosmos—Elyra, the starlight that navigates through darkness, a beacon for those seeking light amidst the shadows."

Lila's smile, bright and unguarded, shone with a warmth that rivaled the dawn. "Elyra... it suits you perfectly."

From that night forward, The Dark embraced the name Elyra, a symbol of their evolving friendship, a name chosen in the sanctuary of shared nights and whispered stories, a guiding light in the tapestry of the night.

CHAPTER FIVE

SECRETS IN THE SHADOWS

As twilight surrendered to the velvet embrace of night, Lila sat enshrouded in the soft glow of her room, a quiet anticipation in her heart. The hours spent awaiting Elyra's visit had become her cherished ritual, each night a promise of new revelations.

The darkness coalesced gently into Elyra's form, her arrival as silent as the whisper of shadows. "Good evening, Lila," she greeted, her voice a soothing melody that seemed to fill the spaces between the stars outside Lila's window.

"I've noticed," Elyra began, her tone shifting to one of gentle inquiry, "your eagerness for our meetings, yet you stay confined within these walls. Why not venture out?"

Lila's fingers paused in their idle dance along the fabric of her blanket. She looked up, her eyes reflecting a mix of longing and resignation. "I wish I could," she confessed, her voice barely louder than the sigh of the night wind. "But my strength wanes quickly, like a candle in the breeze. The world beyond these walls demands more energy than I can muster."

Elyra's expression softened, empathy radiating from her in waves. "I see," she murmured, acknowledging the depth of Lila's silent battles.

Lila's gaze fell, a shadow crossing her features. "My mother is my anchor in this storm, understanding without words. My father, though... he sees not the struggle, only the stillness, mistaking my quiet for a lack of desire to soar."

With a tenderness that seemed to blanket the room, Elyra reached out, her touch a fleeting comfort. "Your spirit shows a strength that many never find," she offered, her words a beacon in Lila's moment of vulnerability.

As the night wore on, their conversation meandered through the landscapes of heart and mind, a shared journey under the watchful gaze of the moon. Yet, Elyra's eyes often strayed to a corner of the room, a silent testament to a sorrow or secret held close to her heart. Lila noticed but chose respect over curiosity, a silent acknowledgment of the spaces even friendship hesitates to illuminate.

In the sanctuary of their shared nights, a profound kinship had blossomed, nurtured by tales of wonder and the comforting presence of the other. Yet, the mystery of Elyra's unspoken thoughts lingered, a delicate thread woven into the fabric of their growing bond.

Lila's curiosity, tempered by patience, held a quiet space for Elyra's revelations, whenever they might come. For now, the joy of their companionship, the exchange of dreams and stories under the blanket of night, was a treasure beyond measure, a light against the backdrop of an ever-deepening curiosity.

CHAPTER SIX

SHADOWS OF WAR

In the stillness of the night, a sudden disturbance shattered the calm. Elyra, breaking her usual respect for Lila's rest, urgently woke her.

"Lila, wake up, now!" Elyra implored, her voice laden with urgency.

Blinking away the remnants of sleep, Lila's heart pounded with fear. "What's happening?" she stammered, panic rising. "Elyra, you're scaring me. What's wrong?"

Elyra shared the somber truth. "The daily routines your parents and the townsfolk engaged in were not just for peace. They've been fortifying the town, bracing for an attack. An army is advancing on your city, bringing the horrors of war."

Lila felt the words strike her like a physical blow. "War? Here? But my mother...she wouldn't have..." Her objection trailed off into stunned silence.

Elyra's gaze mirrored the depth of the tragedy. "Your mother was valiant in defense of the town, but she fell in battle. She's gone."

The reality of her mother's death enveloped Lila in a suffocating wave of grief. Tears streamed down her face as she grappled with the unbearable truth. "No...it can't be..." she sobbed.

Elyra wrapped her arms around Lila, offering solace. As Lila's shock began to wane, a haunting question emerged. "And my father...?"

Elyra's expression darkened. "I saw your father flee at the first sign of conflict, abandoning his comrades and family in a desperate bid for self-preservation."

Feeling utterly abandoned, Lila crumbled under the weight of her shattered world. It was then that Elyra offered a beacon of hope. "Lila, there is a way to escape this pain, a chance for you to transcend this tragedy," she said. "I can change you, save you from this fate. It's a transformation, a new beginning amidst the shadows and the light."

Lila looked up, a fragile hope flickering in her eyes. "A way out? But how? What change could possibly shield me from this sorrow?"

Elyra met Lila's gaze with a promise of untold possibilities. "I hold a power that can alter your essence, offer you a refuge from the grief that engulfs you. This path will demand courage, and the choice to embrace it is yours alone."

In the depths of her despair, yet intrigued by Elyra's mysterious promise, Lila saw a sliver of light in the darkness. She reached for Elyra's hand, ready to embark on a journey of transformation, their destinies irrevocably intertwined.

CHAPTER SEVEN

THE ETERNAL CHOICE

The room was filled with a tense anticipation, punctuated by the distant rumble of unrest and the occasional gust rattling the curtains. Elyra's gaze was heavy with the gravity of the moment, her next words set to reveal a transformative possibility for Lila.

"Lila," she began, her voice a blend of softness and resolve, "I hold the power to change you, to endow you with abilities akin to my own. But be aware, this transformation is profound and irreversible."

Lila's mind swirled with a tempest of grief and unanswered questions in the wake of her mother's death. So much loss, so much pain - yet Elyra's words hinted at a chance for something new, an opportunity for transformation that could reshape her very existence.

With reddened eyes but an undercurrent of fragile hope, Lila leaned closer to her ethereal friend. "Change me?" she asked, her voice barely above a whisper yet burning with tentative curiosity. "How... how so?"

Elyra paused, her face a portrait of compassionate solemnity. "Into a being who moves in sync with the night's celestial rhythms, eternal and fluid as moonlight. Not a creature of darkness, but a sentinel guardian of the twilight realm."

"Eternal?" The profound idea seemed to both fascinate and unsettle Lila. "You mean, to become... immortal?"

With a solemn nod, Elyra confirmed, "Precisely. Yet, immortality bears its own weighty burdens. It gifts you the bearing witness to ages unfolding, but it also means enduring the heartache of outliving those you hold most dear."

A heavy silence enveloped Lila as she absorbed the enormity of Elyra's words. So much to consider - the implications of everlasting life, both wondrous and sorrowful. That thought sparked a new thread of curiosity.

"If I accept this destiny... we would remain together throughout, wouldn't we? Eternal companions on this vast journey?"

Elyra's features softened then, her eyes reflecting a sincere, reassuring warmth. "Yes, our bond would forge an enduring connection transcending ages. We would navigate endless adventures, crafting a kinship to withstand both epochs of joy and periods of sorrow."

Elyra's eyes held a gentle seriousness. "Remember, our friendship doesn't chain you to my side. There will be moments when our views diverge, and it's in those moments, we must be ready to embrace our differences with grace."

Lila pondered this truth, the weight of such consequences giving her pause. That contemplation soon sparked another question. "And the daylight... how does it affect your existence?"

A lilting chuckle escaped Elyra's lips, akin to the night's breeze stirring leaves. "The sun does not bring me harm. Rather, it merely heralds my time of respite, as my spirit is eternally bound to the velvet embrace of night. My reality is a perpetual dance between shadow and lunar luminance, forever following the moon's course while eluding the sun's rays."

Lila felt the profundity of her choice fully bear down then. So much to risk, to gain, to potentially lose. "There is... much to consider about this path, Elyra," she murmured, her voice nearly swallowed by the weight of the distant conflict's encroaching echoes.

Extending her hand in solidarity, Elyra provided a steadying presence amidst the uncertainty. "Take whatever time you need, Lila. This choice rests solely upon your shoulders. But regardless of the decision you make, I vow to stand by your side, now and forever."

As they remained together in the room's sanctuary, the looming sounds of the approaching strife serving as a harsh counterpoint, Lila began to envision her life as an intricate tapestry. Before her lay an array of possible futures, each potential path representing a single thread woven into the grand design of eternity - a tapestry carrying the promise of untold stories, of second chances, of a new beginning that would irrevocably alter her destiny.

CHAPTER EIGHT

SHADOWS REBORN

The room was enveloped in a profound silence, a testament to the gravity of Lila's imminent decision. Moonlight streamed through the window, cloaking the room in a spectral glow that pulsed with anticipation, as if the very essence of the night held its breath for her verdict.

With conviction resonating in her voice, Lila declared, "Elyra, I've made my decision. The thought of facing this vast world alone, devoid of the companionship you've offered, instills a fear in me far greater than the prospect of immortality."

A complex tapestry of emotions danced across Elyra's face—joy intertwined with a trace of sorrow. "Lila, are you certain? This step is irreversible. There's no returning to the life you once knew."

Lila's resolve shone brightly, undimmed. "The bonds of my past life have unraveled. In you, I've discovered a beacon of hope, a sense of belonging that signals the dawn of a new era. My destiny is interwoven with yours."

Elyra's smile, radiant and comforting, illuminated the shadowy confines of the room. "Our meeting was fated, Lila. Hand in hand, we'll traverse the corridors of time, our spirits linked through every epoch."

As they clasped hands, a gentle luminescence enveloped them, mirroring the moon's tranquil glow. Lila underwent a transformation, subtle yet momentous, her being echoing Elyra's celestial elegance—her hair shimmered with the luminosity of the stars, her eyes deepened to wells of nocturnal clarity. The room's brighter elements receded, revealing an altered reality.

Embraced by an ethereal buoyancy, Lila felt liberated from the earthly shackles that had once bound her spirit. She drew a deep breath, each inhalation richer and more life-affirming than the last, as if the very air of the night bestowed vitality upon her.

"Welcome to your new beginning, Lila. In our realm, the night is an ally, and the shadows, a sanctuary," Elyra murmured, her tone a soothing serenade.

Surveying her surroundings with newfound awe, Lila perceived the world through a lens cleansed of former apprehensions. "Elyra, I am eternally grateful. You've bestowed upon me not merely a fresh chapter but the treasure of your companionship."

With these words still hanging in the air, Lila felt a compelling urge, an unspoken invitation from the world beyond her window. Moved by an instinctual pull towards the embrace of the night that was now her domain, she approached the window, pushing it open to let the cool night air caress her face. The scents and sounds of the night, once distant and foreign, now greeted her as familiar friends.

Standing at the open window, the moon's silver light washing over her, Lila paused for a moment, drinking in the sensation of freedom and the vast expanse that awaited her exploration. Then, with a determined breath, she hoisted herself up and carefully climbed through the window, her movements graceful and assured. Her bare feet made contact with the grass below, still warm from the day's sun, grounding her in her new reality.

For the first time in years, Lila found herself standing under the open sky, bathed in the moon's silver light. The vast canvas above, sprinkled with stars and endless possibilities, beckoned to her with promises of mysteries and adventures yet to come. With Elyra suddenly at her side, she took her first steps into the night, each breath a vow of the countless nights they would now share, delving into the boundless beauty of a world seen anew.

Chapter Nine

EMBRACE OF THE NIGHT

As Lila's feet met the cool grass, grounding her in the night's embrace, she paused, a sense of awe washing over her. With Elyra by her side, a figure of strength and mystery, Lila felt the night welcome her, an ancient friend beckoning her into its fold.

Lila drew a deep, deliberate breath, letting the crisp, invigorating night air fill her lungs to the brim. She held it there, a moment suspended in time, savoring the sensation of the night wrapping around her, a tender embrace vast and intimate. Then, with a gentle exhalation, she released the breath, a slow sigh that spoke of liberation and a vitality that coursed through her anew. This breath, a simple act, felt like the first true breath she'd ever taken, each molecule of air a spark of the night's endless energy.

"I can finally breathe," she whispered, her voice a blend of wonder and relief. The night around her responded, a silent affirmation of her newfound place within its embrace. The darkness, once an unknown to be feared, now unveiled itself as a realm of endless possibilities, its secrets hers to discover.

Elyra's presence, reassuring and constant, offered silent encouragement. "The night has always been a part of you, Lila. Now, you're truly home," she said, her words carrying the weight of timeless wisdom and the promise of adventures yet to be written in the stars.

Lila turned to face Elyra, her eyes wide with wonder. "I never imagined the night could feel so... alive," she breathed, her voice trembling slightly with excitement. "It's like I'm seeing the world for the first time, truly seeing it."

She took a tentative step forward, her bare feet sinking into the cool, dew-kissed grass. Each blade seemed to whisper its welcome, tickling her skin with a gentle caress. Lila marveled at the sensation, so different from the cold, hard floor of her room. She wiggled her toes, relishing the earthiness that now connected her to the world in a way she had never experienced before.

As she walked, Lila found that her steps were surer, more graceful than they had ever been. The weakness that once plagued her body had vanished, replaced by a strength that flowed from her core to the tips of her fingers. She stretched out her arms, marveling at the way her skin seemed to glow in the moonlight, a soft luminescence that marked her as a child of the night.

"What now?" Lila asked, turning to Elyra with a smile that lit up her face. "Where do we go from here?"

Elyra's eyes sparkled with mischief and promise. "Wherever the night takes us, Lila. The world is ours to explore, to experience in ways you've never dreamed of."

Lila's heart swelled with anticipation, a thrill running through her at the thought of the adventures that lay ahead. She reached out, her fingers intertwining with Elyra's, a gesture of trust and companionship. Together, they stepped forward, ready to embrace the mysteries and wonders that the night held in store for them.

CHAPTER TEN

RECKONING SHADOWS

In the weeks that followed her transformation, Lila knelt before her mother's grave, fingers gently tracing the soft petals of night lilies unfurling in the moonlight. To the townsfolk, these delicate blossoms thriving in darkness seemed an anomaly, but for Lila, they symbolized undying love and remembrance.

Elyra stood vigil, a reassuring presence as they upheld their ritual of tending the grave, planting lilies, and sharing memories. Lila's mind drifted, recalling her mother's soothing lullabies, the tender embrace, and the adoring gaze. Tears welled, not of sorrow but gratitude—for those fleeting moments and her newfound life beside Elyra.

Fingertips stilling on the petals, Lila turned to Elyra, her voice barely audible. "My father... is he alive?"

Elyra's eyes flickered briefly before a small nod. "He lives."

Relief and apprehension flooded Lila. So long embraced by night, by Elyra's constancy, facing her father seemed a surreal notion. Yet a part of her yearned for this confrontation, to extinguish the turmoil he stoked.

"I must see him. Find closure." Her words strengthened. "Leave the past behind."

Concern etched Elyra's features. "Can you stay measured? His actions deeply scarred you."

Lila fell silent, feeling the sting of abandonment, his failure to understand her fragility. But clinging to that anger would only shackle her newfound self. "I can let go. To truly move forward, unbound."

Studying Lila's resolute eyes, Elyra nodded, a faint smile tugging at her lips. "Then I shall guide you to him. But remember, you are no longer that frail girl. You are night's child—resilient, powerful."

Gratitude shone in Lila's smile as she rose, casting one last look at the lilies swaying farewell.

Their path wound far, starlight and purpose illuminating each step, until reaching a secluded corner where decay and abandonment hung like specters. An old, derelict dwelling crouched there, walls whispering tales of ruin.

In the dimly lit confines of the derelict house, where shadows danced like phantoms across the crumbling walls, Lila found her father, isolated and diminished. The room was pierced by the faint glow of a single candle, its light a stark symbol of his dwindling existence. This feeble flame, flickering in the overwhelming darkness, mirrored the man himself—once a beacon in Lila's world, now a guttering candle struggling against the smothering gloom of his own making.

Coalescing from shadow, Lila materialized before him, night's incarnation. Transformation's crucible had burned away former frailties, leaving only an accusatory strength. Her father, paralyzed by primal terror, could not move, breathe, or speak.

"You left us," Lila's words sliced through the tomb-like silence. "Abandoned your family to suffering's clutches while you fled." Her gaze scorched him. "Is this the peace you coveted?"

His eyes, haunted saucers, gave no answer nor atonement. Only cowardly stillness in the face of his treachery laid bare. "Why so still now, father?" Lila continued, her voice a gentle but piercing inquiry.

Lila drifted closer until the faltering candle's flicker danced between them. An oppressive quiet descended, a canyon of recriminations and lost chances. Then, with a voice carrying contemplations of night's essence yet laced with night's harshest bite, a single damning word:

"Coward."

A breath expelled—soft as the tenderest zephyr yet cutting like a banshee's wail. The candle's fragile light winked out, plunging them into perfect oblivion. From that abyss rose her father's scream, a sound of purest horror and desolation swallowed by the infinite dark.

Outside, under the night's eternal embrace, Elyra waited, her glow a beacon of calm in the turmoil of the night. As Lila stepped into the open, the tension in her shoulders eased, her posture relaxed—a visual sigh of relief. There was no need for words; the softening of Lila's eyes conveyed her message clearly: her father remained unharmed, merely shaken by the encounter, left to contemplate his actions in the solitude he had chosen.

Together, they turned from the dilapidated house, its darkness now a closed chapter in Lila's life. The act was not one of retribution but of liberation, an emotional unburdening that allowed Lila to leave behind the weight of her past grievances.

This transition was not merely an end but a beginning. Freed from the shadows of her former life, Lila now walked alongside Elyra, stepping confidently into the night that had once harbored her fears. Their path, illuminated by the subtle glow of their companionship, promised a journey of exploration and understanding, a shared adventure into the depths of the night, unshackled and renewed.

CHAPTER ELEVEN

JOURNEY THROUGH THE NIGHT'S VEIL

As twilight deepened, Lila, filled with anticipation, stood next to Elyra, the embodiment of the night's enigma. "The shadows are our roads; the night air, our conveyance," Elyra whispered, her voice carrying the promise of unseen worlds on the cool breeze.

Elyra extended her hands, and the shadows coalesced around them like a dark cloak. Her hair, a cascade of night itself, enveloped them in an ethereal veil. For a moment, they hovered at the boundary of the visible and the unseen before dissolving seamlessly into the embrace of the night.

Lila experienced the journey not as a passage through space but as a flight through the essence of night. Blending with Elyra, she felt as if they were gliding from one shadow to another, their silent passage marked by the invisible threads that weave through the heart of darkness.

Their first stop was beneath the shimmering canvas of the Aurora Borealis. The air's chill, a stark contrast to the warmth of their shadowy passage, invigorated Lila, awakening within her a sense of life and vitality. Elyra, a silhouette against the night, stood as a testament to the ageless dance between light and darkness. Lila marveled at the beauty of the celestial display, feeling a deep connection to the mystical forces at play.

From the frozen north, their path led them to a secluded grove, hidden deep within the ancient forests of Asia. Here, under a canopy where moonlight danced through the leaves, Lila felt her soul connect with the velvety darkness. With Elyra guiding her, they explored the grove, their presence so light that the natural world around them remained undisturbed. The night air, rich with the earthy scent of the forest, was a symphony of natural sounds that resonated with the very core of Lila's being. In this moment of tranquility, they found solace in the beauty and serenity that only the heart of night could reveal.

Next, in the silent expanse of the desert, they paused to reflect. Here, the night revealed itself in a different form: vast, open, and unadorned by the trappings of the world. Lila, exploring her newfound abilities, reveled in becoming mist, her essence spreading out over the sands and caressing the cool earth. Elyra's guidance was a gentle force, pulling them across the dunes under the protective gaze of the stars. Lila felt a sense of freedom and limitless potential as she merged with the desert night.

The culmination of their journey brought them to the edge of a silent, mirror-smooth lake, reflecting the stars like a vast, still canvas painted with the light of distant suns. Here, the boundaries between water and sky blurred, with Elyra's shadows crafting a secluded space along the shore. Lila, drawn to the tranquil beauty of the scene, experimented with her ability to shift between forms. The gentle lapping of water against the shore harmonized with her movements, a reminder of the delicate balance between the natural and the supernatural.

As the first hints of dawn began to lighten the sky, they stood together, united by the shared mysteries of their nocturnal journey. "Through shadow and mist, we've traversed the night," Lila mused, her voice echoing the depth of their experiences.

"And so we will continue," Elyra promised, her form beginning to merge with the fading darkness, "for our journey through the night knows no end."

With that, they retreated back into the shadows, their forms blending with the night as it receded. This journey had been more than a mere exploration of places; it was a journey into the heart of their bond, a shared voyage into the boundless realms of darkness, ever ready to unveil the next mystery that lay hidden in the night. Lila knew that this was just the beginning of their adventures together, and she looked forward to the many secrets the night would reveal to them in the future.

Chapter Twelve
THANK YOU

From the shadows where we dwell and in the whisper of the night wind, we, Lila and Elyra, extend our deepest thanks to you for journeying with us through the pages and sounds of "Lila & The Dark." Your presence alongside us has brought our tale from the quiet shadows into the moonlit realm of shared experience.

This narrative, spun from the essence of twilight and given life by the luminescence of the moon, was lovingly crafted and shared by Chris Ross. We invite you to visit crbooks.ink, our online sanctuary, to explore more of our stories and connect with our journey.

To all our readers and listeners, your engagement with our journey illuminates our path forward. If our tale has touched your spirit, please share your reflections with Chris Ross. Your feedback is the beacon that guides us through the endless night.

For those whose paths we cross, remember, that the night holds more than just shadows, and in its embrace, we find the tales yet untold. Our journey does not end here; it merely whispers of beginnings, of stories waiting to be discovered in the hush of twilight.

And as we part, a gentle reminder: in the realm of night, we see all. So tread the path of shadows with care.

Just Remember...

WE...CAN SEE...

IN THE DARK.

Farewell for now,

Lila and Elyra

The End

ABOUT THE AUTHOR

Chris Ross, from Erin, Tennessee, is an emerging author who finds beauty in exploring the unseen, creating stories that challenge us to look beyond appearances. His journey into writing was encouraged by his friend Sharon, who gave him the support and motivation to finally share the stories he had envisioned for years. **"I've always wanted to write a story based in my hometown,"** Chris shares, "and with Sharon's encouragement, I was finally able to bring my ideas to life."

Since childhood, Chris has been captivated by fantasy. **Living near a library, he would often sneak off to escape into worlds of magic, history, and adventure.** These early experiences inspired his love for storytelling, and he brings this passion to his works. His latest book, *Lila & The Dark*, was inspired by the saying, **"Nothing in the world is just black and white."** Through this novel, Chris encourages readers to challenge their perceptions and see beyond the surface. His favorite line from the book reflects this belief: **"The unseen need not always be feared. Darkness often harbors wonders invisible in daylight—like the stars that reveal themselves only at night or the dreams that visit your slumber."** This quote, he explains, is **his way of reminding readers that everything in life needs to be seen from different perspectives.**

Chris's debut book, *Moving Out*, launched his literary journey, followed by *Lila & The Dark*, which brings fantasy to life in a unique exploration of fear and friendship. Currently, he is working on *The Shadows Beneath: The Harper Reed Mysteries*, a suspenseful mystery that promises to unveil even more hidden layers in familiar places.

Outside of writing, Chris finds joy in spending time with his wife, Katrice, and their children, Ethan and Rebecca, whose love and support inspire his creative journey. He invites readers to explore his works and join him on his journey through crbooks.ink.

COMING SOON: CITY & SHADOWS

Dear Readers,

I'm excited to share that the journey into the mystical world of Lila & Elyra continues beyond Lila & The Dark. Writing their story has been a truly joyful experience, and I'm eager to explore their adventures even further.

The next chapter, titled City & Shadows, is already in progress and promises to delve deeper into their immortal wanderings. Prepare for big surprises, long-awaited answers, and fresh layers to Lila and Elyra's timeless saga.

In this upcoming book, you'll embark on a thrilling journey through the shadows of an enigmatic city. Expect enchanting encounters, mystical revelations, and new characters—both allies and adversaries—as Lila and Elyra's paths intertwine once more.

I'm pouring my heart and soul into crafting this next installment, and I invite you to stay connected for updates on its progress and release. Your continued support means the world to me, and I can't wait to share this new adventure with you.

Until then, keep dreaming. The shadows hold countless tales waiting to be discovered.

Yours truly,
Chris Ross